SNOWBOARDING
on
MONSTER MOUNTAIN

Eve Bunting

Cricket Books
Chicago

Library of Congress Cataloging-in-Publication Data

Bunting, Eve
  Snowboarding on Monster Mountain / Eve Bunting.— 1st ed.
    p. cm.
Summary: Callie tries to hide her extreme fear of heights on a snowboarding trip to Mammoth Mountain with best friend Jen, who Callie fears may prefer the friendship of new girl and skilled snowboarder Izzy.
  ISBN 0-8126-2704-0 (cloth : alk. paper)
  [1. Best friends—Fiction. 2. Friendship—Fiction. 3. Fear—Fiction. 4. Snowboarding—Fiction.] I. Title.
  PZ7.B91527Sle 2003
  [Fic]—dc21

                                                          2003009981

To our snowboarders—
Tracy, Dana, Tory, Erin, and maybe Shane
—E. B.

Chapter 1

Tomorrow I'm going to Mammoth Mountain for the weekend with my friend Jen and her parents. We're going there to snowboard. The very thought scares me half to death.

But I'm going.

People think if you live in California you don't get snow, only sun. They're wrong. We live in Pasadena, California, and we get rain in winter. Around Christmas we can see snow, way up on Mount Baldy. Higher still, in the Sierra, the snow is really deep.

"Snowboarding is so neat, Callie," Jen says, all smiling. "It's like zooming down a humongous slide."

Uh-oh! I'm not happy zooming down any kind of slide, and a humongous one sounds awful. Actually, I'm terrified of heights.

"Can you stop when you're going down on your snowboard, if you're, like, halfway?" I ask Jen. "Are there brakes?"

Jen laughs. "Oh, Callie! You are so funny! There aren't brakes. But you can stop any time you want by turning the nose of your board uphill and twisting." She twists herself to show me. "You'll learn how when you have your lesson. You won't want to stop, though. It's so great."

Right now we're sitting on the couch in Jen's apartment in front of the TV. Jen has tapes of the 2002 Olympic snowboarding in Salt Lake City. We've already watched them twice. Americans won all three medals—the gold, the silver, and the bronze—in the halfpipe event. A girl, Kelly Clark, won the women's halfpipe gold. Jen knows every move by heart.

"Watch Kelly get big air here," she says excitedly.

I've discovered "big air" means jumping so high on your board you look as if you're flying. They're snowboarding in a pipe thing that seems to be made

of ice or maybe hard snow. They go so fast. It looks so scary I'm getting sick just sitting here, watching.

"Kelly's my hero." Jen nudges my shoulder. "Don't worry, Callie. That's not the kind of boarding we'll be doing. We'll just glide down the slopes. There's nothing to it."

I laugh a fake laugh. "Thank goodness," I say.

Jen gives a little shiver of excitement. "I can't wait for tomorrow."

I nod "me, neither" and cross my fingers behind my back.

We're going to Mammoth for three long snow-boarding days. Jen and I are out of school for winter break, and her parents have taken time off work. Everyone's jazzed, except for me. I'm actually feeling sick to my stomach, but I know I'm not coming down with something. It's just those nerves leap-frogging inside me.

I've been asking myself why I'm going to Mammoth tomorrow and I've been answering myself. Fortunately, nobody can hear my answers except me. First, of course, I'm going because Jen asked me. Because we're best friends. Secondly, and this is the secret part, because if I turned down the invitation she would probably ask Isabella Garcia to go in my place. Isabella's pretty new in our school. Her dad was transferred from Colorado to a bank in Pasadena, right in the middle of last semester. Being new can be a total bummer, but it doesn't seem to be hard for Isabella. She's totally hot, with long, black hair. She laughs a lot, and I have to admit she's nice. She has this little black beauty mark on her cheek, and some of the girls thought it was so cool that they began putting eyebrow pencil beauty marks on their faces, too. I didn't. Jen didn't, either.

"It's really funny," Izzy said. She'd told us to call

her Izzy. All her friends do. "It's so funny," Izzy said. "Because when I was little I used to try to scrub my black mark off. I thought it was so ugly." She spread her hands. "But it wouldn't come off, so I'm stuck with it."

We laughed, and Jen said, "Here." With a yellow wash-off pen she drew petals around the mark to make a daisy.

Right from the beginning I'd known that Jen and Izzy were going to get along great, and that gave me a frightened, sinking feeling. What about me? Jen and I have been best friends since preschool, just the two of us. If I'm honest I have to confess that it didn't take me too long to wish Izzy hadn't moved to our school. Which I know probably means I'm insecure and a rotten person, too.

Izzy knows how to snowboard and ski. Well, she *did* live almost all her life in Colorado.

"I like snowboarding better," she told Jen. "You don't have to keep worrying where your legs are."

Jen laughed. "Exactly. I bet you're good."

Izzy shrugged. "I guess I'm O.K."

If Jen had asked Izzy instead of me to go to Mammoth with her, I wouldn't have been surprised. Hurt, definitely. But not surprised. I even suggested it, to show how generous I am. But Jen said, "Well, it would be great to have Izzy, too. But my dad said just one friend. So of course I chose you. We're tight on room in the car. He said if there was another kid going she'd have to ride on the roof. And the ski racks are up there."

I smiled happily. Yeah! She chose me. And it wouldn't be all snowboarding at Mammoth. Jen said we'd be in a cabin and we'd have a big, roaring fire and we'd toast marshmallows and play Monopoly and Scrabble. All that sounded great. But there'd still be that gigantic, old, snow-slick mountain waiting for me.

So here I am, smiling happily on the outside, but my insides are not smiling at all.

Tomorrow we're going snowboarding.

Chapter 2

I'm spending the night at Jen's because we're leaving real early in the morning. It's a five-hour drive to Mammoth Mountain. We're lying on Jen's bed before dinner, reading *Tuck Everlasting*. It's cool that we're both reading the same book at the same time. We do that a lot. Mine is from the library, but Jen got hers for her twelfth birthday last month. There's a movie of the book, too, but we decided not to see it, at least not till we've finished reading. Maybe not even then. We check where we are in the story as we go along and we stop at the end of each chapter to talk about it. I'm faster so I sometimes have to stop so Jen can catch up. I lie and stare at the ceiling and think how nice this is and wish we could just stay here and forget Mammoth Mountain. The good smell of lasagna cooking drifts up from the kitchen. The two bedside lamps make circles of shadow-light on the ceiling.

When the doorbell rings, I hear Jen's mother cross the hallway and then I hear her say, "They're in Jen's room, hon. Go on up." And I have a sudden sense of foreboding.

My foreboding is right. It's Izzy.

"Hi, guys!" she says, coming in all smiling.

We sit up, and she rushes across to hug us both. We're all into hugging.

"Oh cool!" She looks at our books. "That's supposed to be so great. Can I borrow it when you've finished? I haven't read it yet." She beams at us. "And then, after, we can all talk about it."

"Sure," Jen says. "We're more than halfway through."

I smile falsely. Now Izzy's going to butt in on something else that's ours. Probably there'll be three of us on the bed reading next time.

She holds up two CDs. "Look what I have. Two Beatles albums. My Aunt Marlene sent them. You're bringing your Discmans in the car with you, right?"

Jen nods. "Definitely."

"I listened to them last night," Izzy says, "and they're super. You'll know all the songs. They'll help pass the time."

Jen makes room on the bed, and Izzy plonks down between us. I move over reluctantly so she can have more space. She's there between us. It seems like a bad omen. I can see myself in the mirror above Jen's dresser and I look like a crab. What's the matter with me? As if I don't know. It starts with a J

and rhymes with "tell us." I don't even want to say the nasty word to myself.

Izzy pulls out the CDs to show us. "These have all their great songs. You can each listen to one and then trade."

"Wow, thanks," Jen says, and I nod. "Thanks."

Our snow gear is over by the bedroom door, ready for us to pick up in the morning. Jen's board is red with a lightning bolt zigzagging across it. Mine, which is borrowed from her cousin Melissa, is blue. I glance at it quickly and away. Those boards are bigger than I'd imagined they'd be. My gosh, they're almost like surfboards.

Izzy gets up and goes over to them. "O.K. if I look at these?"

"Sure," Jen says.

Izzy runs her hand down Jen's. "Oh, they're both Burtons. I like these. I had a Burton Feel Good before I got my new one. They're perfect for beginners."

Jen giggles and gives me a nudge. "That's what we are—no kidding."

"You're not, Jen," I protest, but Jen says, "Oh yes I am. I'm definitely no expert."

Izzy is still inspecting our boards. "These are

good," she says. "They're soft with lots of flex. You'll have no trouble, Callie."

I think she sounds condescending, but she's probably just being kind.

"Gosh." Jen tilts her board so it's more secure against the wall. "I wish you were coming with us. You could give us both some pointers."

Izzy makes a face. "I'd love to be going."

Should I say, "You can take my place"? That would be such a relief. But it would be that awful worry again. She'd be with Jen, two snowboarders, doing fun stuff together for three whole days, getting to be best friends. I bite my lip. It's too late anyway. Instead I say jokingly, "Jen's dad said one of us could ride on the car roof."

Izzy grins. "I'm not sure I want to go that badly."

"Tell us what your new board's like," Jen asks.

"Oh, it's a Rossignol Diva. A lot of the hot boarders use Divas. Not to say I'm hot. But I'm looking forward to trying it. It's longer and stiffer. Divas are supposed to be really responsive. I can do a 360 on it, no problem. My dad ordered it for me on the Internet. It was so funny. I had to answer all these questions—my weight, my height. My boot size." She holds up one of her feet and giggles. "It was so embarrassing. My feet are huge for my height. Even the computer was amazed."

"Your feet are not even slightly huge," I say, trying hard to be nice. "My big brother wears a size 13, and my mom says his feet are still growing. And look how humongous our boots are."

We all glance across at them. Mine are Melissa's. They fit me perfectly, worse luck. I'd thought if they didn't I'd have an excuse to just go up to Mammoth Mountain and watch. But Jen's mom said, "Don't worry, hon. If they don't fit right, we can rent a pair for you. That's not a problem." No use trying to get out of it by pretending they cramp my toes.

"And then Dad had to click on all these other questions," Izzy went on.

"Like what?" That's me asking, all enthusiastic.

"Oh, if I was a beginner or intermediate or what. And then there was stuff like, could I link turns and make it down most runs in style. Dad kept checking 'yes.' He decided that the Diva was the best board for me."

For something to do, I get up and brush my hair in front of the mirror. I'm wishing and wishing that

I wasn't afraid of heights. And that I could snow-board and ride a Diva down the mountainside, making all those runs in style and astonishing everyone with my perfect 360s, whatever they are. And that I had a beautiful velvety birthmark on my cheek, just like Izzy's.

Chapter 3

Jen's mom asked Izzy to stay for dinner, but she said she couldn't. Her grandmother and grandfather were coming to their house tonight, and she needed, actually wanted, to be there.

"Have a great time, you guys," she tells us, and we all hug again.

"Thanks."

"What a dear girl," Jen's mom says. "Next time we go to Mammoth, maybe we should rent a bigger car or a van and take all three of you."

"That would be awesome," Jen says.

Miserable, horrible me says nothing.

After dinner we watch Jen's tapes of the 2002

Olympic snowboarding one more time. By now I know all the moves by heart. Of course, knowing is not the same as being able to do them.

Jen sighs. "Do you know what they say? When you get big air, jumping isn't as hard as landing. But I figure it's all hard. I might try, though, this time. You move your weight to the back of the board so the tip comes up and then you leap and the board comes with you."

"And you're partway down the mountain?" My heart hammers with horror at the thought.

"Sure," Jen says.

"Do we have insurance?" Mr. Webster asks mildly from behind his newspaper. But he doesn't sound too worried.

Jen laughs. "We'd better." She slumps back. "Callie? Do you think, maybe at the next Olympics we'll be watching Izzy winning gold?"

"It's possible," I say. "I bet she's really great."

Jen closes her eyes. "She'll be on the stand and the American flag will go up and the anthem will play and there she'll be, holding the flowers." Her voice is dreamy.

Her dad looks over the top of his paper. "Now that's a leap if ever I heard one."

Jen turns to me. "Don't worry, Callie. You'll just be gliding down those slopes." She holds her arms wide, as if she's flying. "Nothing fancy."

I laugh a tinny, fake laugh. "What a relief!"

When we've watched the tapes all the way through again, we try on our gear. First you put on the boots and buckle them up, then you slide your feet into straps called bindings and lock yourself in. Now you're stuck to the humongous board. My mouth is dry as dirt.

"What if we want to get out of them?" I ask. "I mean, when we're moving?" I'm thinking mountain, slope, high, slippery . . . me on it.

"These are quick-release buckles," Jen says. She shows me.

"But even so," I mutter. I'm not sure they'll release quickly enough for me.

"Don't worry, sugar," Jen's mom says. "A couple of lessons and you'll get the hang of everything. Jen just had one lesson, and she was ready to go."

But that's Jen, I think.

We are in bed by nine because we have to be on our way so early. Jen goes to sleep quickly. There's a night-light in our room so we won't fall if we have

to get up, and I can see our clothes on the chair, all ready for morning.

I lie there, my heart doing little fluttery things every time I imagine the mountain. I may have a heart attack before I even get there.

My mom and dad advised me to turn down Jen's invitation. My mom had taken both my hands in hers.

"Honey, this could be torture for you," she said. "Why don't you just tell Jen the way you feel? It's always better to be truthful. She'll be happy to have you with her, even if you don't go up on the mountain. Maybe there's a skating rink? You could both go skating."

I shook my head. "This is all about snowboarding. But, Mom, I can do it. I'm sure I can."

Mom didn't know about Izzy and THE BIG THREAT. She'd be ashamed of me if she guessed that was my main motive. I didn't want to imagine the way she'd look at me.

Dad was working on his computer. He turned around. "Callie? Do you remember when we went on vacation to Seattle? You said you were certain, positively certain you'd go with us to the top of the Space Needle. You said you were determined."

"I know. And then I couldn't." I gnawed at my thumbnail. "But this is different. I was way younger then. And I really, really want to do this. I'm resolved!"

"Resolved is just another word for positively certain," Dad said. "You told us in Seattle that you'd be O.K. since you were there with us. And then you were *not* O.K."

I remembered crying that day and backing away from the elevator that carried the brave people to the top. It was raining. I remembered that, too.

"But this time I'll be with Jen," I said desperately. "I can be myself with you. I can be a baby if I want. But this time I can't. I'll be with her."

I stopped, and my mom said softly, "And with Jen you can't be yourself? I thought you were friends."

I shrugged and I didn't answer.

You don't understand, I thought. With Jen I have to hide it. How awful to have her start wishing she'd brought Izzy instead of me. And be planning on bringing Izzy next time and leaving me behind. I don't think I could stand it.

Chapter 4

It's just past dark in the morning when we leave. The mountain closes at four, and because of the five-hour drive everyone's in a hurry. I try to imagine how you close a mountain. There's a lot of stuff about this that I don't know.

We pile our gear into the car. I watch Jen's dad load chains into the back. "We might need them to get through the snow," he says. Her parents' long skis are strapped to the racks on the roof, and there's barely room next to them for our two boards.

I pretend to measure the roof and make a joke. "Definitely no room for another girl," I say.

Jen and I are in the backseat surrounded by backpacks and duffels that won't fit in the trunk.

Jen squeezes my hand. "I'm so glad you're coming with us, Callie."

I'm glad, too, because I'm with my very best friend in the whole world. Just the two of us. And those icy slopes are still far away.

Jen and I talk about school stuff and then we talk about Kelly and the guys who won the halfpipe. "They're really young," she says. "Ross, the one who took the gold, is twenty-three, but Danny's only nineteen. He won the silver, remember? The pros say he's the most inventive rider in the world."

I nod, trying to remember which one he was. When we'd watched, they'd all looked just about the same in their helmets and riding gear.

"J.J.'s twenty."

I nod again. "They were so great."

We listen to Izzy's CDs.

Jen can't read in the car. She says it makes her eyes go wobbly and her head hurt, so I read Tuck out loud. At first I read softly so as not to disturb her parents in the front seat. But her dad says, "Hey, Callie! We can't hear you properly. Speak up!"

Jen's parents are so cool. Well, mine are, too.

After a while we stay quiet, looking out of the car windows as we rush along. First there's the desert with these big cactus plants that grow in strange shapes. They look as if they're spreading their thorny arms wide, as if they're balancing.

I nudge Jen. "Maybe they're sandboarding." I hold my own arms wide the way Jen had shown me snowboarders do, knocking over the Monopoly game that's wedged between the two backpacks.

We go through Red Rock Canyon, where the cliffs are made of sandstone and you can see caves tunneling through them. The early sun is turning them this beautiful bright red, like a crayon drawing. It looks like an abandoned village, lived in once by cave people. I'd like to get out and explore, but we're headed for the mountain. And it closes at four. Snow like sprinkled flour dusts the sides of the road and powders the pine trees. It truly is beautiful.

We stop for breakfast in a little town called Olancha. The restaurant has a wooden veranda, and hens cluck in a side yard. Two honest-to-goodness cowboys in cowboy hats and with red kerchiefs tied around their necks are eating eggs at the counter.

"Aren't they neat?" Jen whispers.

I nod. "I can't believe it. Do you think they rode in on horses?"

"Probably," Jen giggles. "Hi-ho, Silver!"

We eat quickly, although we get through a pile of food. Scrambled eggs and homemade biscuits with gravy, or honey if you have a sweet tooth. While Jen's parents are paying the bill, we examine a rack of postcards. They're almost all of the mountains of Mammoth. Oh, heavens! Here's one that shows that big, awful, snowboarding one.

"Hey!" Jen says. "Let's buy this card and send it to Izzy. Or take it to her, anyway." She looks at me. "Maybe that would be mean, though, since she couldn't come with us."

I shrug. "No. I think she'd like it."

Jen pulls out another card. "I'm going to get this one for myself, too. I like souvenirs."

I smile to show what a good idea I think that is. But I don't buy one for me. When I'm home, I'm hoping to put this mountain behind me.

The cowboys are still eating. It would be great to hang out and watch them leave on their horses, if they have horses. But we still have a couple of hours' driving to do.

For a while we play "What was your happiest day ever?" and "What was your most embarrassing moment?"

Jen tells about the time she got locked in the bathroom stall at school. I tell about the day I dropped my tray in the cafeteria, right in front of John Forsythe, who is definitely the hottest guy in our school. But I don't tell about my truly most embarrassing moment. Nobody knows about that except my mom and the teacher and some kids who were there.

I'll never forget, even though it was a lifetime ago. Actually, I was in third grade. It was summer vacation. Jen was in Florida with her parents, and I wanted to go swimming in the Rose Bowl pool. I liked the swim lessons. But on the last day, we got to go up on the low board and jump off. I think it was supposed to be a treat, or a reward. From down below it didn't look that high. I forced myself to climb the metal ladder because it would have been mortifying to be the only swimmer who didn't jump. But when I stood on that board, with the blue water below me, I could see everything. First the space below the board and then more water space all the way down to the tiled bottom of the pool.

My stomach heaved. There was no way I could leap off into that nothingness.

I stood, quivering, at the very end of the board. Behind me kids were lined up, shouting, "Jump! Jump!" And I couldn't. "Go or I'm going to push you," some horrible guy behind me yelled, and I backed up, swaying so hard I'm not sure why I didn't fall. From below I could hear Christine, our swim teacher, shouting, "Move over. Let her through." And then, "If anybody tries to push her, he'll answer to me."

I crowded past. One boy moved his shoulders and elbows up and down and went, "Cluck, cluck, cluck." I didn't care.

The kids on the ladder had to get down, one by one, to let me off. It seemed everybody in the pool area was watching me, in my blue swimsuit and the swim cap they made us wear if we had long hair. I wanted to disappear. I can feel my face getting red now, just remembering.

My big brother, Tom, goes to San Diego State University. He called that night, the night of the diving board, and I talked to him. I can always talk to Tom.

"I hate being this stupid," I said, and I tried not to whimper.

Tom was quiet. Then he said, "Do you know what I'm afraid of?"

"Probably nothing." I grabbed a tissue and wiped my eyes.

Tom lowered his voice. "Clowns."

"Clowns?"

"You know, in circuses. The guys with the red noses and the big red mouths and feet like paddles. There's always hair like straw poking out from their hats, and they think they're so funny. But they're not."

I began to giggle. "I think they're funny."

"See?" Tom asked. "One time Mom took me with her to the opening of a new supermarket, and they had a clown. I ran and hid behind a stack of canned baked beans. And I wouldn't come out."

Now I was *really* giggling. "How old were you?"

"Five. Maybe six. But I'd still hide behind a stack of baked beans if a clown came near me today."

"You wouldn't."

"I would."

My brother is so nice.

I stare out of the window now. Beside me, Jen snores a little snore.

The snow is deeper here, piled high along the sides of the freeway. Mountains sparkle white in the sun.

"Gotta get the chains on," Mr. Webster says, and he and Jen's mom get out. I ask if I can help, but they tell me to stay warm. I can feel how cold it is as soon as they open the door.

Jen wakes and stretches. "Chains on. Must be getting close!"

There are higher mountains here, their tops icy and veiled with clouds.

"Are those the mountains we'll be going down?" I can hardly get the words out. Please, no, I think. They're so HIGH.

Jen gives me a big, happy smile. "Not yet, but soon."

I squinch small in my seat. I'm thinking, a clown's not as bad as a mountain. I'm wishing Tom was here.

It's just a few minutes later that Jen clutches my hand. "Look!" she breathes. "There it is!"

I look.

Mammoth Mountain! It's mammoth, all right. It's a monster!

Chapter 5

We turn up a narrow road that winds among trees. Our tires sink in the snowy ground. And there's the cabin. It's made of wood, and snow lies white as frosting on its roof.

"We're here!" Jen's blazing with excitement.

We climb out of the car, and cold hits me like a hammer. Snow comes up to our ankles.

I shiver. "Brrr."

Jen laughs. "You think this is cold? Wait till you get on the mountain."

No way is the cold going to be the worst thing for me. If I ever make it onto that mountain, which seems impossible.

We haul all the stuff in from the car and dump it on the kitchen floor. There's new linoleum with funny little sparkles in it, but the cupboards are old and slanted, like they're tired after hanging there for all these years. It's as cold inside as out. Jen's mom finds the bread and peanut butter and strawberry jelly that she's brought, and Mr. Webster brings in the ice chest from the car so we can have milk.

We eat standing up, gobbling the sandwiches. I wish there was some way to slow things down.

"It's ten after one already," Mr. Webster says. "Let's get into our gear."

In no time we're bundled up in everything except our helmets and we're heading for the mountain. My mind scuttles around. It's going to start getting worse from now on. I don't see any escape.

We find a miracle space close in among a million cars and trucks. This is like getting parked for the big Christina Aguilera concert we went to at Staples Center. Dogs bark at us from the backs of pickups, big, woolly dogs that look as if they belong in the snow. There are men and women and kids in jackets and great clumpy boots everywhere I look.

The mountain looms over us. I try not to see, but it's hard to ignore. It's so gigantic.

We pick up our gear and head into a big, square building. Jen's dad buys tickets, which we clip to our jackets. There's an outside cafeteria crowded with skiers and snowboarders. I listen to bits of their conversations.

"It's slushy in the bowl!"

"The powder's great at the top."

They clunk around in their enormous boots, their parkas hanging open, their passes dangling from their pockets. It's all like a big party . . . with food. I smell chili. And hot stew. I feel sick.

I make myself look at the mountain. The slopes are alive with small figures careening down the side like surfers on some humongous ice wave. It's almost a traffic jam. The chairlifts swing up, up, up, heading for the sky. Gondolas like silver-and-glass boxes glide soundlessly on their cables. Bordering the slopes are great, tall pine trees, heavy with snow.

We slather on sunblock, and Mrs. Webster gives us each a tube for our pockets.

Beside me, Jen takes a deep, satisfied breath. "Oh, Callie. This is going to be the most perfect day."

I'm freezing, inside and out. It's amazing that I'm not hunched up here, blubbering.

"Let's go get you into the class," Jen's dad says, and he takes my arm. We walk toward a sign that says, "Ski School." I hadn't realized cousin Melissa's snowboard was so heavy and awkward. The ski school has a net, like the net in a tennis court, all the way around it. And, oh joy! The class must be at ground level. We're going to be on a slope that's so gentle I have to look carefully to see if it actually slants at all.

Jen waves as she leaves. "I'll come back and see how you're doing."

The instructor is young. He looks like one of those Olympic snowboarders Jen and I watched so many times. But he can't be. His name is Rudi. Mr. Webster talks to him for a minute, and they both look at me. Then Mr. Webster comes over and says, "You're in good hands, Callie. We'll meet you back here when your lesson's over."

I'm so happy that I'm going to be down here on this smooth, snow-packed earth all afternoon that I give him a beaming smile. "Great," I say.

Four other kids are getting lessons, too. There are three boys who look like third or fourth graders. Two of them seem to know each other and stand close together. Then there's a girl my size. She's wearing a red knitted cap and she has a red zit, big as a pea, on her chin. I don't stare at it because I know that would make her feel bad. For a minute I think of how big a difference there is between a glowing red zit and a black beauty mark. It's actually not fair.

Rudi says we're a mixed bunch. Usually he has kids that are all about the same age. "But variety is the spice of life, right?" he asks. His smile is wide as a jack-o'-lantern smile, and his eyes crinkle up.

He asks us our names and prints each one on a card that he slides in a plastic holder and pins on our jackets. He asks our ages.

"How old do you think I am?" he asks then.

"A hundred and ten," one of the boys says and giggles.

"Hey!" Rudi is fake offended. "I'm twenty-one."

"So," the kid says, "I can't help it if you look a hundred and ten."

It's not hard to see he's going to be a smart mouth all the way.

There are strange-looking gray carpet strips going up and down our small slope. Rudi has us sit on them while he shows us how to park our boards when we're not using them, kind of on their sides so they won't roll. "When you're up on the mountain you don't want to rest your board and then see it slide away from you, taking a few other snowboarders out with it," he says. He explains to us about courteous boarding. All the rules and regulations.

A part of my mind is doubtful that I'll ever need to know. Will I really and truly ever be snowboarding down a steep mountain? I try to at least courteously listen.

He has us get off the carpet, stand up, and buckle one foot into the snowboard bindings. The board feels heavy and awkward, this big planklike thing stuck on the bottom of my leg. But at least my other foot is safely on the ground.

"Don't worry about how clumsy it feels," Rudi says. "You'll get used to it. Besides, when you're boarding you'll have two feet on the board and you'll be graceful as birds."

A chicken hawk, I think, trying not to shiver.

We set off down the gentle slope to the bottom, pushing and sliding. It's easy.

Then we crawl back up the carpet strip, like crabs, our boards still attached and clunking along with us.

"Now," Rudi says, "you're going to go down with one foot still buckled in. But this time you put your other foot up on the board behind the front one."

We're trying, falling, tumbling, lying on the snow more than standing on the boards.

Rudi shouts encouragement.

"Isn't falling fun? It's all part of the game." He helps us stand.

"Not if you fall on the real mountain," the other girl, Lori, grumbles, and Rudi says, "That'll happen, too. When you do, you get up, move out of the way so no one crashes into you, and keep on riding."

A tiny girl and her mother are watching us from outside the fence. The little girl is stuffing snow in her mouth.

Rudi calls out to her, "Don't be eating our snow, sweetheart. We can't spare any."

I like Rudi a lot. But if I ever have to really go on the mountain, he won't be with me. But I won't think about that now. I'll just listen to him and try to do this part right.

"Keep the noses of your boards pointed forward," he says. "We're not into riding backward."

He's laying a pole flat on the snow almost at the bottom of our slope.

"This is going to be easy," he says. "First we buckle in both feet, then we ride down and jump over the pole. You just jump, that's all, and the board comes with you. You all know how to jump, right?"

We're not sure. I'm not sure. What would happen if we said, "No. We're not even going to try that"?

Nobody does. It's not that Rudi is strict or mean. He's just not the kind of instructor you'd ever say no to.

I crash into the fence after I jump, but at least that stops me from going farther and plowing into the crowd on the other side of the netting. I feel totally helpless with both feet buckled in. I feel trapped. But I can take the board off. I do, and flex my legs, each in turn.

"Oh man." Lori is lying on the snow, and I help her up.

"Did you ever feel like an upside-down turtle?" she asks me.

We carry our boards and walk up the carpet strip together.

I slide my hand over cousin Melissa's board, brushing off the stuck-on snow, and I realize something. I could do this, if I didn't have to do it down a mountain. It's not the snowboarding or the falling that scares me. It's that I would have to stand up there, up high, and push and let myself go into that awful, white drop. I remember the space below the diving board the time I tried to jump. Sky above me, then water below. Sky above me now, and icy abyss below. I hear this strange sound and I realize that I've given a little whimper. Quickly I look at Lori, who's sitting next to me, but she hasn't heard.

Jen comes down once to visit. Her cheeks are red as strawberries. Her nose, too.

"Oh, Callie! I'm so stoked," she says. She's standing outside the fence; I'm inside. "It's wonderful up there on the mountain. Just wait. You'll see. And, Callie! My dad carved Cornice today. He says maybe by the next time we come up I'll be good enough to try it."

"What?" I ask. "What's that?"

She points back up the mountain. "Cornice is one of the expert runs. It's a Black Diamond. Really, really hard. I can't wait to tell Izzy what Dad said."

Izzy, of course, would know all about Black Diamond runs. She could probably do them in her sleep.

"I jumped over the pole," I say. "Three times. And I didn't fall."

"Great!" Jen's enthusiastic. "Now you know how to ride and jump."

"But I'm definitely not ready for the mountain yet," I add, in case she has ideas.

"You will be soon," she tells me.

Want to bet, I think. "This year, next year, some-time, never," I joke, acting as if I'm pulling petals off a daisy and blowing them into the air.

Jen smiles. "You are so funny, Callie."

The thing is, I'm not being funny at all.

Chapter 6

When the lesson's over, Rudi tells us we all did splendidly. He says he'll see us tomorrow. "You're all registered for two lessons," he tells us, glancing at a clipboard he has left on a pile of packed snow. "Tomorrow we'll move on past the preliminaries."

"Will it be here? In the same place?" I ask breathlessly.

"Well, tomorrow we're graduating to Sesame Street," he says, pointing behind us and to the left, away from Monster Mountain.

We all turn to look.

Sesame Street is another smooth little hill, maybe

a little steeper than the slope we've been on today, but not much.

"Glory, glory hallelujah," I mutter under my breath.

Beside me, Lori asks, "How hard can something called Sesame Street be?"

"Not as hard as it might be," I say semiecstatically. I can see that tomorrow is not going to be bad at all.

"I hope you're not too disappointed that you're not graduating all the way to the top," Rudi says. "But you have to walk before you can run. And you have to learn before you can perform."

"It's O.K. with me," I say.

He grins. "Pretty soon you'll own that mountain."

I let myself turn in the other direction and look at it.

Nobody has ever owned Monster Mountain, and nobody ever will.

It's four o'clock, and the slopes are emptying.

And here comes this great woolly creature, like an abominable snowman heading in our direction. Real little kids wouldn't be too sure about him, but it's easy to see he's just a person, dressed up, like the mascot at the high-school football games.

He ambles over, one great, furry paw outstretched.

"Give me five," he says and holds his paw to the three boys. The two called Jeff and Kingsley seem to know each other, and they whisper a lot. "I hear you guys are going to be awesome snowboarders." Their gloved hands are swallowed up, one by one, in his great paw.

"Yeah, yeah, we're going to be whiz experts," Kingsley says and rolls his eyes, which I see already is his favorite way of showing he's cooler than anyone.

"I'm Woolly Mammoth," the monster tells me and Lori. "I'm the spirit of the mountain."

"How do you do," I mumble, and Lori pumps his paw and says, "Hi. Nice to meet you."

I'm glad Lori's in the class with me. She's touching her zit, probably hoping the cold will have made it disappear.

"I get those sometimes," I tell her. "Zits Away works pretty well."

"I know. But not on a monumental one like this."

"Try rubbing snow on it," I suggest. "Can't hurt."

"Thanks," Lori says. "It's worth a try. See you tomorrow."

Jen and her mom and dad are coming toward me.

"Did you have fun?" they ask. "Did you like it?"

"It was great," I say. It would be rude to say anything else. After all, they paid for my lessons. "I'm not actually sure how much I learned," I add cautiously.

"Probably more than you think." Jen's dad puts his arm around my shoulders. "How about some hot chocolate in the lodge?"

"And croissants?" Jen asks.

One day over, I tell myself. And I'm still alive.

The lodge is too warm and too crowded, people jostling people carrying trays, or groups visiting each other's tables. The talk and laughter are loud enough to split eardrums, but it is a totally happy noise.

I look around and wave to Lori, who seems to be with her parents. Jeff and Kingsley are at a table opposite us. They're throwing popcorn at each other. Then I see Wes, the third kid. He's pushing his way over to them. Behind him at a table is an elderly couple, watching him and smiling. I see him scrabble up some popcorn kernels off the floor and toss them at Jeff. Jeff looks around. He grins, then hooks an empty chair with his foot and pulls it toward them. Wes smiles a big, happy smile, and he's just about to sit when Kingsley puts his feet up on the empty chair and glowers at him. He gives Wes a real dragon look, then turns the dragon look on Jeff. There's no way he's going to let Wes sit with them.

We grab a table and park our boards and skis beside us. I wave. "Hey! Wes!"

Wes turns, then comes slowly toward us. "Hi," he says shyly.

"Hi, yourself. Everybody, this is Wes," I say.

"Want to sit a minute?" I ask. "This is my friend, Jen, and her parents."

"Hi." Wes hesitates. "I better get back to my grand-parents. I'm staying with them for a week." He gives a little wave in their direction.

"You did really good today," I say.

"Thanks." He fidgets with the toggle on his red jacket.

Jeff and Kingsley are staring across at us.

"Are those your two pals?" Jen asks.

"They're in our snowboarding class," I say.

And Wes adds, "They're in my class at school, too. I told them I was coming up here over winter break." He bites his lip. "Jeff said they'd see me up here, so I thought, maybe . . ."

I knew what he'd thought. That they could do stuff together. That they could hang out. But Kingsley wasn't having any part of that. I wondered why. Wes seemed like a really nice little guy.

"So see you tomorrow," I say, and Wes nods. "See you."

When he can't hear, I point over at the other two boys. "Wes wants to be tight with them so bad. But they won't let him."

"That stinks," Jen says.

"They haven't realized yet that you can't have too many friends," says Mrs. Webster. "'He who has a thousand friends has not a friend to spare.'" She glances at her husband. "Who was it said that, Jim?"

"I haven't a clue," he says.

I look down at my empty hot chocolate cup.

There's something that I just saw happen, something I just heard, that I need to think about. But not now. There are too many worries in "now" already.

I stare at the big lodge window. It's actually a wall of glass. Mammoth Mountain outside fills it, like a giant painting. A few stragglers are still coming down the slope as if they want to get every minute out of the day before it ends. I wish I could get over the feeling that the mountain is waiting for me. That there's no way to escape it. I tell myself that for me the danger of the first day is over. Tomorrow will be O.K. But then there's the day after that. Somehow I'll have to get through that day, too.

Mr. Webster has gone for refills on the hot chocolate. He's juggling a cardboard tray with four cups, which he sets on the table. We pass them around. Then, still standing, he raises one of them and says, "To Callie, brand-new snowboarder."

Everybody drinks. Even me.

Chapter 7

We have a big fire that night and eat bowls of chili and toast marshmallows. It's just the way I imagined it would be, all cozy and friendly. But by 8:30 we're yawning and ready for bed. Everyone's tired, and tomorrow is going to be a full day.

Jen and I are in the teeny back bedroom. There are two bunk beds opposite each other. They look as if they've been made from chopped-up tree branches. We spread our sleeping bags on top of the patch-work quilts. Mrs. Webster has brought a plug-in night-light from home, and there's a lamp on the stool between the beds. We're close enough to touch.

Jen's propped up on her pillow, writing the card she bought for Izzy. "I'm sending this from both of us," she says. "'Course, I'll really just have to give it to her when we get home. But this way she'll know we were thinking about her. What should I say?"

"I dunno." I open my book at the bookmark.

"Wish you were here," Jen says, writing. "That's really lame. But still, it's true."

I give a little grunt that could mean I agree, or not.

"Great snow," she says, still writing. "Love, Jen and Callie."

She snuggles down. "I'm too pooped to read."

"Me, too." I lean over and switch off the lamp.

The night-light shines on the wooden ceiling and on the skimpy curtains, which are white with red skiers chasing each other from top to bottom. I wonder, do they ever catch up?

Mr. Webster pops his head in to see if we're O.K. and blows us each a good-night kiss.

"Your dad is so nice," I say. "Your mom, too."

"I know." Jen lowers her voice. "Izzy told me something really sad about her parents."

She lowers her voice even more, the way you do when you maybe shouldn't be telling something at all. "She says her mom and dad may be going to get a divorce. She says they're hoping that coming here to California may help them get together again. But Izzy says she doesn't think so. She says they fight a whole lot. They try not to let Izzy and her little sister hear them, but they do hear, and it's awful."

I lie there, jealously picturing Jen and Izzy having a private conversation. Where was I? I didn't know they got together and had these kinds of best-friend talks.

"What else did Iz say?"

"She says she hopes she doesn't ever have to choose between them, you know, which one she'll live with if they separate. She loves them both so much."

"That's horrible," I say. There's a little bump on the tree-wood frame of my bed, and I rub it with my finger. Maybe it was a branch once, and somebody cut it off. What if it starts to grow again, and I wake up covered with little twigs and leaf sprouts?

I think about how sorry I am for Izzy and her little sister. But at the same time, I'm wondering how many of these conversations Jen and Izzy have had. Or is this all the same one?

We lie quiet.

"Do you think Izzy would mind that you've told me?" I ask.

"No." Jen's voice is sleepy. "She likes you a lot. She's glad she has us for friends."

I nod, and my head shadow bobs on the wall, so faint that it almost isn't even there. But I'm thinking, Izzy didn't tell me. I rub the little tree bump and rub it and rub it. So what if it grows? Dad once had a worry stone that someone brought him from China. It was smooth as glass, and you were supposed to rub it to soothe your worries. Maybe this is my worry bump.

"Do you think it's snowing outside?" I ask Jen, trying to sound perky, trying to get away from the thought of Izzy being sad and me being mean.

"Maybe," Jen says.

I don't think you can hear snow falling; it's so soft and gentle. It could be drifting down right now. It could be blizzarding, even. I lift my head off the pillow, listening, and I suddenly get a really hopeful thought.

"What if it snows really hard?" I ask Jen. "If it snows tomorrow, we won't be able to go up on the mountain, will we?" I hug my arms around myself and close my eyes and silently whisper, snow, snow, snow. Because although I'm only going to be in Rudi's class again, and Sesame Street doesn't seem that big a problem, I'd rather just stay safely in the cabin where you can't even see the mountain unless you stand outside on the front path. And I wouldn't do that. I don't even want to look at that mountain. I hug my arms around myself and close my eyes and silently whisper, SNOW, SNOW, SNOW.

"Don't worry," Jen mutters. "We'll be up there even if it blows the biggest storm in the history of Mammoth."

"Oh," I say, and I think, oh, oh, oh!

I can tell she's almost asleep.

It's so silent. I listen to myself breathe. At home, when I'm in bed, there's the noise of cars passing on the street outside. Sometimes I hear birds calling to each other. Thinking about it makes me feel lonely and homesick. I want to run away. There are too many scary possibilities and too many bad thoughts. But how could I run from here? The snow would swallow me. Maybe I couldn't even find the road in the dark. And there's no traffic. Everybody's asleep, happy, dreaming about the mountain and carving Cornice. There wouldn't even be a kind truckdriver on the road to pick me up. At school, after the holidays, everyone would be talking. "Did you hear about poor Callie Kruger? She froze to death in a snowdrift."

And I can't seem to get rid of the guilty thoughts. I don't want to look at them. They're about me. The little kid, Wes, keeps pushing himself into my mind. I shove him back out. He was so hurt. Those boys were so mean. Especially Kingsley. Am I that mean to Izzy? I am, inside myself, even if I cover it up. And then Mrs. Webster saying what she said about how Jeff and Kingsley hadn't learned that you can't have too many friends and how great it would be to have a thousand, or something like that. I feel like crying, which is so dumb.

"Wish you were here," Jen had written to Izzy. I'm pretty sure she's asleep, but I ask anyway. "Do you really wish, I mean, all that much, that Izzy was here?" I want to add, "Instead of me," but that wouldn't be fair. What could Jen say?

"Well, it would probably have made her feel better," Jen says sleepily. "To be with us. And she's so nice. Besides, we all get along so well together. It would have been fun to have her ride with us. But . . ." Her voice is so full of sleep now that I can hardly hear her. "But tomorrow I'll have you to ride with." She yawns a big, gaspy yawn. "There may even be new snow."

I'm instantly wide awake. "What do you mean you'll have me to ride with tomorrow? You won't. I'll be having my lesson."

"Only in the morning," Jen mutters. "Your lesson's only for half a day. In the afternoon we'll be on the mountain together."

I sit straight up, bunched in my sleeping bag like a snail in its shell. Only half a day? I think my breathing has stopped. I can't even hear it anymore.

Chapter 8

We're up at the mountain by ten the next day.

"Have fun this morning," Mr. Webster calls to me. He's already on his way to the big chairlift.

"See you at twelve," Jen says and squeezes my arm. "I can't wait."

I can.

I take my board and cross the snow to the ski school at the sign marked "Bunny Crossing." Rudi's there already, behind the low fence, talking to the three boys.

"Wait up, Callie," Lori calls from behind me, and I see her running awkwardly to catch up, her goggles pushed on top of her head, her boots slipping and sliding in the snow, her board banging against one knee. This morning she has a small, round Band-Aid covering her zit.

"No better?" I ask.

"It looked so much like a towering inferno this morning that I decided to hide it and give you guys a break."

Rudi is waiting for us. "Ready for another great adventure, girls? Good to be alive in the high country, huh?"

"Hi," I say to Wes, and he gives me a little grin. Jeff nods in my direction and half smiles. Kingsley ignores me.

"Everybody pay attention," Rudi calls. "Today we're going up on the chairlifts."

"What?" I gasp. Worse and worse.

"Only a little way," he says. "This is a small lift. It just goes to the top of Sesame Street." He waves a hand toward the top of the gradual slope that's closest to us. "A cakewalk. Getting on the lift is easy, but there are things you have to know."

I'm watching the chairlift closely as he talks. The chairs are in pairs. They don't seem to go very high. It might not be too bad.

"We'll get on two by two, like the animals boarding

the ark. O.K.?" Rudi grins at us, that stretched-out, easy smile. "So we'll walk together to the lift and then pair off. Lori, you and Callie go together. Wes, you go with Kingsley. I'll be with Jeff."

"Hey!" That's Kingsley's angry voice. "I don't want to go with Wes. I'm with Jeff."

"O.K., O.K., whatever," Rudi says, and he punches Wes on the arm. "It's you and me, kid."

I feel like pushing Kingsley down and smashing a handful of snow into his face. He doesn't care if he hurts Wes's feelings. I would never be nasty like that to Izzy or anyone. I don't think. But, without meaning to, I'm imagining Izzy and Jen and me up here, getting on the chairlift, Izzy and Jen together, me in a chair by myself. Maybe I'd be just as obnoxious as Kingsley. But probably I'd be quiet, hurting inside, madder than ever at Izzy for butting in between me and my best friend.

Rudi gives us instructions, how to get on the chairlift and how to get off.

"Wes and I will be on the first empty chairs that come along. If you need a hand getting off at the top, we'll be there to help you. The thing to remember is to move out of the way quickly. The chairs behind you are still in motion as they make the loop to come back down, including the one you just got off. You don't want to get clobbered."

I interrupt. "You mean, ride away from the chair with just one foot in the bindings?"

"Yep. But you can set your other foot on the board behind that front one. The way we did going down the ski school slope. Everybody understand?"

"Sure," Kingsley mutters.

"Sure," we say.

"O.K., then, let's boogie. Follow me."

We go behind him, like ducks in a row, except that ducks don't have one foot attached to a snowboard. There are some other skiers and boarders in line ahead of us already, and pretty soon a few behind us, too. I watch the line in front get smaller. I watch grownups and kids swing themselves into the chairs as they reach the front. There's a sort of rhythm to it, the chairs never stopping. I have this crazy thought that the chairs don't care who gets on and who gets left behind. It's not their problem.

"Here we go," Rudi says over his shoulder, and he and Wes are safely on.

The chairs sway a little, jiggle as they keep on going up. Jeff and Kingsley go next. I think I'm a little disappointed that they board perfectly.

And then we're on, too.

"All right," Lori breathes.

It's probably pretty if you sit here and look around. I know there are those beautiful snow-covered pine trees. I know the sky is blue, and the clouds high and fluffy white. I don't look around. I keep my eyes fixed on the back of Kingsley's red jacket in front of me. Once I look down by mistake and I can't breathe. I give a little gasp. The snowy ground moves slowly beneath us. I tell myself it's not that high, not that bad. In some places it's only about two feet below our dangling snowboards. But in

some it's six feet or more. I don't want to think about that. I'd like to close my eyes, but I can't. What if I missed the place to get off and went swinging back down? And had to come up again.

"Rudi and Wes are off," Lori tells me. "Jeff and Kingsley, too."

"Us," Lori breathes, and I wait for the right second and swing myself down.

"Perfect," Rudi calls and then, "Kingsley, get yourself out of Callie's way."

Kingsley doesn't move fast enough. We collide and roll over, fortunately away from the lift and the others getting off.

"You turkey!" he says to me as we sprawl in the snow. And then it's a dream come true for me as I pick up a handful of snow and rub it over his face.

He splutters and gasps. When I look up, I see Jeff and Wes standing together, and they're both grinning.

Good!

Rudi's right there.

"See what she did?" Kingsley splutters, and Rudi says, "Yeah. Quit it, Callie." He pulls me up and brushes the snow off my jacket and pants. "And I think I heard you call her a turkey," he tells Kingsley. "You didn't get out of the way like I told you to.

O.K., lesson learned. Everybody follow me over here. Now we're going to do some serious riding."

I give Wes a thumbs-up, then stand with the others at the top of the gradual slope that is Sesame Street. It's not that scary. It really isn't. Rudi may still need to give us a little push here to get us going. My stomach plummets at that thought.

"We did good," Lori says, beaming.

"Not bad," I agree. Then I ask, "Do you have a watch? What time is it?"

Lori takes off a glove, peels back her sleeve, and says, "It's ten to eleven."

An hour and ten minutes before we quit and head back to the lodge. Another half hour or so to eat, and then . . .

Rudi kneels in front of each of us in turn to make sure we're buckled in, tight and secure.

"Everybody ready to go?" he asks.

Sure I'm ready to go, I think. Ready to go home, that is.

Chapter 9

I ride, fall, get up, ride, slide, tumble, get up.

I'm going down Sesame Street, but not the way I've seen other snowboarders go down.

Rudi's ahead of us, waiting at the bottom of the slope. "Remember? You have to walk before you can run. And you have to learn before you can perform," he says with his wide, encouraging smile.

Lori goes up with me on the chairlift on the second run.

"What time is it now?" I ask her.

"Ten after eleven. I guess time goes fast when you're having fun."

I'm not sure if she's being sarcastic or not.

"It's going too fast," I say. "I wish there was a way to make it stop."

Lori smiles. "I know what you mean. I like the lessons a lot, too. And I'm beginning to think I'd like to be a real snowboarder."

It's a good thing she hasn't picked up on what I meant about making time stop. Or go backward.

"Soon we'll be up there," she says. "Look!"

Our chair swings alarmingly as we turn to inspect the mountain.

"It has to be just the same, though," Lori says uncertainly. "Only higher."

"Definitely higher."

We're still staring at it. For me, it's hard now to look away. My eyes seem glued to the peak, as if I've been hypnotized. Not that I've ever been hypnotized. There it is, soaring above everything in the world, cloud-capped, cloud-swept. Sun polishes the lower slopes. It is magnificent and terrifying. Skiers and snowboarders glide down. "Like birds," Rudi had said.

I lick my lips, which are sore and chapped, and immediately the cold dries them out again.

"Watch it, Callie. We're almost at the top," Lori says, and we get ready to jump off.

I do better on my second run. And better still on

the third. Partway down the third, I actually stay long enough on my board to ride for at least thirty seconds with one arm stretched out and my hand gracefully pointed. And for those thirty seconds I feel like a real snowboarder.

At the bottom I see Lori. But she's not standing with the others. She's sitting on her board with her leg stretched out and she's undoing the lace of her boot. Rudi's kneeling in the snow in front of her.

"What's up, Lori?" I ask.

"I hurt my ankle."

"Is it bad?" I look from her to Rudi.

Rudi gently touches her foot. "She's given it a nasty twist. I think she needs to have it looked at. And there'll definitely be no more snowboarding for a day or two." He looks up. "Is this your dad?"

A man in a black parka and black cap is walking toward us across the snow.

"Don't worry, Dad," Lori calls. "I just tweaked my ankle. I'm O.K."

She looks at Rudi. "Thanks for teaching me. I'm really disappointed that I can't try the big mountain."

I look down at my boot and scuff it around in the snow, making a circle and then another. She means it. She's sorry she can't try out the mountain.

"You will," Rudi says. "You've got the heart for it. I can tell."

What can he tell about me?

Lori's dad talks to Rudi for a minute, and the two of them help her stand.

"It doesn't hurt that much, honestly," she says.

"Let's get you where you can rest it properly," her dad says. "Can you walk?"

"I think so." Lori holds on to his arm, and they start to hobble off.

"I hope it gets better fast, Lori," I call after her.

"Thanks." She and her dad stop. I see he's writing on a scrap of paper, which he comes back and gives me. "Here's Lori's e-mail address. She wants you to keep in touch."

I glance down at the paper. "I'll write to her as soon as I get home. 'Bye, Lori."

"'Bye, Callie."

We watch them cross the snow.

"O.K., then," Rudi says briskly. "The lessons are over." He nods toward the mountain. "Pretty soon you'll be up there, shredding the powder."

"You think we will?" Wes asks.

"I know you will. In time. You were a great class. Now, go get some lunch and then try your wings. You'll be on your little butts on the snow a lot of the time, but you'll get up and get on with it. That's how you learn."

He gives each of us another high-five. "I'll see you around. Good luck, snowboarders."

For a few seconds, being called "snowboarder" puffs me up. It sounds so athletic. So professional. Me, Snowboarder, I think and almost giggle. But then I remember what's going to happen after lunch, and my giggle shrivels up.

I'm standing there, watching Lori and her dad heading for the parking lot. He's taking her home, to rest and keep her foot up, and suddenly my mind fills with a new and electrifying possibility. What if I had hurt my ankle today? What if I had to rest up? Then I could sit in the lodge all afternoon and drink hot chocolate and watch everyone else. I could limp a lot. And then tomorrow I could keep on limping and say how sore my ankle was. I could bring *Tuck Everlasting* and sit in the lodge with my back to Monster Mountain and read and be happy. What a perfect solution!

I'm so overflowing with relief and thankfulness that I feel weightless, like one of Rudi's birds. And I'm not even on a snowboard.

Chapter 10

"**G**oing back to the lodge?" Wes asks me.

"Yep." We carry our boards and walk together. I remember to start limping.

"Practice, practice, practice," Rudi had advised. Of course, he'd been talking about snowboarding.

"What's wrong?" Wes is looking down at my jerky steps. "Did you hurt your ankle, too?"

I hesitate. I'm not good at lying. Sometimes I try to get around a lie without actually getting into it. I'm trying desperately now to think of a nonlying way to answer Wes.

"It doesn't feel too good." It doesn't. Both ankles are aching a bit, probably because of the snowboard bindings.

"That's a bummer," Wes says. "You can hold on to me if you like."

I put a hand on his shoulder and limp along.

Jeff and Kingsley are ahead of us.

"How come you want to be friends with those two, anyway?" I ask Wes.

"I dunno," he mutters. "Jeff's O.K. when he's by himself. He talks to me and stuff. But when Kingsley's around, he changes. It's like Kingsley doesn't want anybody to be with Jeff except him, and Jeff goes along with that." He shrugs. "All the kids in school think Kingsley's real cool. He's the pitcher on our baseball team and . . ."

I interrupt him. "He's not cool at all, even if he is a big baseball star. It's not cool to be mean to someone who wants to be your friend."

The words I just said hang in the icy air as if written there in giant loops and curves. "You'd be a neat friend to have," I mutter. "He's just hateful. And Jeff's hateful, too, if he lets Kingsley tell him what to do."

Wes glances up at me. "That's what my grandma says. My grandpa says he knows the reason Kingsley doesn't want me."

"What's that?" I have a strange foreboding about what he's going to say next, as if the words are going to be very important. I've forgotten to limp and I start again.

"My grandpa says Kingsley's afraid Jeff might like me more than him. Grandpa says that's entirely possible since I'm probably a way nicer guy than he is. My grandpa says Kingsley's probably insecure, and we should feel sorry for him."

Like me, I think.

Wes is looking up at me, waiting for me to say something helpful.

I nod. "I bet your grandpa's right."

"You know what my grandma says?" he asks.

I shake my head.

"She says there aren't too many problems that a chocolate chip cookie can't fix."

"I think that's right, too," I tell him.

We're going up the steps to the lodge now. I let go of Wes and hold on to the rail, limping pitifully. Maybe Jen and her parents are already there, at a table by the window, watching for me.

But they haven't come yet.

"Want to sit with me and my grandma and grandpa?" Wes asks.

"Thanks," I say. "But I'd better just wait. They'll be here in a minute."

I park my snowboard in the rack outside the

door. There's an empty table inside, so I grab it and save the seats with my gloves and helmet. After a minute I drag over another chair and prop my foot on it. From here I can look out, and right then I see them coming, the mountains and trees like painted scenery behind them. Like the card Jen bought for Izzy. The wish-you-were-here card.

"I twisted it on the third run," I mutter to myself, getting my story ready. LIE.

"It hurts a lot." LIE and DOUBLE LIE.

"I won't be able to snowboard anymore today. Probably not tomorrow, either." LIE AND TRIPLE LIE.

I'm suddenly so hot I unzip my jacket and wriggle out of it. Why is the smell of food sometimes so revolting? And the loud talk. It's so noisy, it's making me dizzy.

The three of them are pushing their way toward me.

"Callie!" Jen calls. She's got red cheeks and a red nose in spite of all that sunblock. Her hair is sweaty-looking from being in her helmet all morning. She leans over to hug me. "How did you do today? Was it great?"

I nod.

"I've never known a morning to go so slowly," she says.

"She kept asking me, 'What time is it? What time is it?'" Callie's mom says. "She nearly drove me crazy."

"Well," Jen says, "it's been hard to wait for you, Callie. But now I'm so excited."

Her dad laughs. "Slow down a minute, Jen. Maybe Callie doesn't feel ready for the mountain yet."

"She does. I know she does. Callie and I do everything together." Jen crouches down beside me. "We'll just go on Chair Three. That's an easy run. It's only partway up. Midway."

Mrs. Webster is pulling off her gloves. "Callie, honey. Is there something the matter with your foot? Why do you have it propped up like that?"

I stare at her, at her nice, kind, unsuspecting face.

My mouth forms my first practiced lie, but it sticks somewhere at the back of my throat.

"Oh no!" Jen wails. "You haven't gone and hurt it, have you?"

I think I'm going to bawl. What's the matter with me? How can I even think of lying? But how can I not?

"I was just resting it," I say. "It's fine."

Jen lifts one of my gloves out of the way and sinks down on the chair.

"Thank goodness," she says. "So you'll come up with me?"

I nod, and Jen beams.

I close my eyes. I AM RESOLVED.

"I'm taking lunch orders," Mr. Webster says. "Who wants a hot dog?"

Jen and I put up our hands.

"And could I have a chocolate chip cookie?" I ask.

Chapter 11

We're off Chair Three and standing partway up Monster Mountain on a wide area of snow. Not that wide, though.

It is so cold. My knees are shivering, and I have to clench my teeth to keep them from chattering.

Mr. Webster has gone up on the lift that takes him to the top slopes, but Mrs. Webster is with us, and there are lots of other skiers and snowboarders in motion or getting themselves psyched up to take off. We move close to the edge and buckle into both bindings.

I'm numb.

Maybe I'm paralyzed.

I don't want to even glance at that mountain that drops in front of us, that's just a wall of ice with little puffs of snow blowing across it.

It can't be perpendicular. But close. That's what I'm supposed to go down.

I am resolved, I tell myself. Resolved.

I turn my back to that perpendicular drop and look up.

The mountain rises behind us, as terrible behind as in front.

I'm in this horrifying place, either halfway up or halfway down, and no chance of getting away. I feel like a bug on a mirror.

"Are you O.K., Callie?" Mrs. Webster looks worried. My terror must be showing.

"I . . . I . . ." I know there's no way I can do this. I can't stand up straight anymore this close to the edge. I have to be flat on the snow. I have to be safe.

And then, to my mortification, I discover I've dropped to my hands and knees, my snowboard still clamped to my foot at this odd angle, my hands grabbing handfuls of loose snow as if that's going to stop me from falling down, down into that awful depth below.

I hear Jen's frightened voice that seems to be

coming from somewhere far away. "What's wrong, Callie? Mom, what's the matter with Callie?"

Mrs. Webster's kneeling beside me, and there's someone else, too, someone wearing huge boots. They look so heavy and solid that I grab hold of the nearest one.

"Is she sick?" a man asks.

"I don't know. She seems to be dizzy." That's Mrs. Webster. She's saying my name over and over and rubbing my back.

"It's probably the altitude," the man says. "This altitude can do bad things to you if you're not used to it."

Jen crouches in front of me. "But she was O.K. yesterday."

"I've got my cell phone," the man says. "Should I call the ski patrol? They'll toboggan her down."

I raise my head and let go of my death grip on his boot. "No. No. I'm just not feeling well. Don't call the ski patrol. I'd be so embarrassed. If I can only get . . . off the mountain."

The man releases my snowboard, and they help me stand. I cling to him. He seems so sturdy. He could dig in the heels of those big boots and stop me from slipping headlong into that awful, endless abyss.

Mrs. Webster's saying, "Honey, the only way to get off the mountain is to scramble down on your rear end. Little by little."

"Can't I go down again on the chairlift?" I ask. I'm panting as if I've run the fifty-yard dash. The thought of the chairlift isn't good. But if I know it's going down instead of up, it will be a lot better.

" 'Fraid not," the man says. "I think you can if it's a total emergency. But it's a big deal, and you have to get permission. The chairs go down empty. It would be too dangerous to let anyone ride them. You could tip out."

I swallow hard and pull in my breath.

Stuck. Stuck halfway up Monster Mountain!

The man leans down and peers at my face.

"It's not that hard to scooch down. Honest!"

"It isn't," Jen chimes in. "I've done it lots of times. When I lose my board or something."

"I'll scooch with you, O.K.?" The man unbuckles his own snowboard and slides it into a holder on his big backpack. "It'll be cool. I promise."

I stare up at the bigness of him, at those solid legs and heavy boots.

"Can I hold on to you?" I ask shakily.

"You bet. And I'll be holding on to you." He

looks at Mrs. Webster. "By the way, I'm Tony. I'll get her down. Don't worry."

"I know you will," Mrs Webster says. "I'm really grateful."

"I'm sorry to make such a . . ." I begin and I half turn to look at Jen.

She's crying. "This is so awful, Callie."

"Don't cry, Jen," I whisper. I'm afraid the tears will freeze on her cheeks.

"Let's do it, then," Tony says cheerfully. "Ready?"

I'll never be ready, I think. But I nod.

I tell myself not to look at what's below us as we start, me on my butt, Tony on his, holding my elbow, sliding, spider crawling, inching together down Monster Mountain.

Jen is inching right next to me, and her mom is carrying my board and snowplowing slowly on Tony's other side.

Oh my gosh! This is taking forever. I can't handle it.

"You're doing great, Callie," Mrs. Webster calls.

"You're almost there. See? I told you it wouldn't be that hard," Tony says.

I want to keep my eyes shut, but that's even scarier than having them open, so I half close them and squint. Is it true that I'm almost there? I make myself look. The ground is closer, much much closer. It is true. I'm almost there.

And then, miracle of miracles, we're on flat ground.

I can stand.

A thought flashes into my mind. Once I was knocked over by a wave when I was swimming at Santa Monica beach, and it was terrifying, the water over my head, fizzing in my ears, choking me. And then I got my feet under me and I could stand. I'd always remembered that moment of relief and joy. I'd always remember this one.

I turn to Tony. "Thank you, thank you a million times," I sob. "Thank you, thank you, thank you."

He pats my shoulder. "You're welcome, welcome, welcome."

I throw my arms around his big, bulky waist and kiss his jacket.

Mrs.Webster laughs. "Good grief! I'd better put a stop to this before she starts kissing your boots." Then she says, really seriously, "We are so grateful to you, Tony. I'm sure we could have brought her down. But you're a very reassuring person."

And Jen adds, "Totally! If I'm ever stuck on the mountain, Tony, I hope you'll be around."

That makes us all laugh again, and then Jen's mom says, "Have a wonderful rest of the day, Tony. Happy boarding."

We wave good-bye as he heads for the chairlift.

"He's so nice," Jen says.

I nod. I'm so happy to be safe that I could fly like a bird.

I've heard of travelers who kiss the ground when they come down from a bad airplane trip. I'm not about to start crawling and kissing the snow again, though. I was on all fours long enough up on Monster Mountain. And I've already kissed Tony's bulky ski jacket. That's probably enough.

Jen and her mom begin to fuss around me like I'm the most delicate and precious person on earth.

"I can't believe that happened, Jen," I say. "I'm all right now. It probably was the altitude." I'm already enough better that I realize I'm telling one of my semi-lies. It was the altitude all right. But it was more than that.

"We'll get you back to the cabin," Mr. Webster says.

"No. No," I protest. "Honest, I'm fine. You'd think you'd have to get Jen's dad, and one of you would think you had to stay with me in the cabin, and that would be awful. Just let me sit in the lodge. You go back on the mountain. I don't want to spoil your whole day. I can watch you. I want to."

"Well . . ."

They help me up the steps, though I tell them I don't need help.

We go in the rest room, and I sponge my face and hands. I'm so white I could audition to be the first abominable snowwoman.

They stay with me, getting me tea with lots of sugar, which I sip to please them even though it tastes yucky.

Mrs. Webster knows the woman who takes the cash at the food line, and she promises to keep an eye on me, and I'm to go to her if I need anything.

At last they leave.

They look back at me as they head for the chair-lifts, and I wave cheerfully. "Don't worry," I mouth.

There's such a mixture of relief and embarrass-ment inside me that I can't tell them apart.

I sit by the window. A storm's coming up. Clouds hang black and heavy on the top of the mountain and tangle themselves in dark fingers in the pine trees. It's going to snow hard or maybe rain.

I leave my tea and walk around the lodge. I wonder about Lori's ankle. I don't see Wes or his grandparents or the other two boys. Maybe the three of them are out boarding together. I doubt that, though. Poor little Wes. He's probably still trying to get past Kingsley. And it's not that easy to push in on a twosome if one of them doesn't want you. He should ask Izzy. Or me.

There are racks of cards with views of Mammoth

Mountain and the Mammoth Lakes. I haven't seen any lakes. There are souvenir key rings and refrigerator magnets and coin purses, white and sparkly, shaped like the mountain. I stand in front of the display. There's a key ring with a dangling wooden snowboarder. Her jacket is painted yellow, her pants are bright blue. Her hair is long and black as licorice, like Izzy's.

"How much?" I ask.

The souvenir woman smiles apologetically. "Eight dollars and forty cents. Things are expensive up here. They get you coming and going."

"It's O.K." I unzip the pocket of my waterproof pants and slide out the ten dollar bill my dad gave me when I left home.

The lady drops the key ring in a small Mammoth bag. "Is it for yourself, lovey? A little memento?"

"I might give it to someone who couldn't come," I say. "Or I might keep it. I'm not sure yet."

Chapter 12

They come off the mountain early. The storm is really in now, blasting against the walls of Main Lodge, shaking the snow off the trees.

"You can't even see up there," Mr. Webster says.

Mrs. Webster puts her hand over mine. "Were you O.K.? By yourself?"

"Fine," I say.

"I don't suppose, if it clears up tomorrow, you'd . . ." Jen begins.

"Hush, Jen," her dad says. "We don't want to put poor Callie through that again."

I'm safe. So why do I feel so miserable?

"Isn't there anything you can do for this altitude thing?" Jen asks.

"Yes. Stay off the mountain. And drink plenty of water," her mother tells her. She brings me a paper cup filled to the brim from the drinking fountain.

We inch our way back to the cabin, the car up to its hubcaps in snow.

The plan had been to go to a restaurant called Gomez for a Mexican dinner, but once inside we don't dare venture out again. So we have canned soup and the rest of the peanut butter on crackers.

The fire is great. We crouch around it and play Trivial Pursuit and tell ghost stories, but not ones that are too scary, in case of bad dreams.

By 9:30, Jen and I are in our sleeping bags. It's not quiet outside tonight. The wind is roaring, and every now and then there's a soft plop as snow falls off our roof. In the small glow from the night-light, I can see across from me the hump that is Jen. We haven't talked about what happened on the mountain. Maybe her parents suggested that it wouldn't be a good idea. But she has to be wishing she'd had Izzy with her instead of me.

"I'm sorry . . . about today," I whisper.

"You couldn't help it," she says.

"I really couldn't."

I lie there, listening to the wind that's like a train roaring by. After a while I can tell Jen's asleep.

I don't like my thoughts.

There's not enough light to read. Which is a bummer, because reading would help me to not think about myself. I slide out of my sleeping bag and find the key ring I bought. When I shake it, the snowboarder sways gently. She could be a girl on a Rossignol Diva, carving Cornice. If I do give it to Izzy when I get home, it will mean something. It will actually mean a lot.

It's cold. I slither back into my sleeping bag and cuddle down and pretty soon, in spite of the train rushing by outside, I'm asleep, too.

I wake up with a jolt. There's a loud crackle and then a crash. Someone is screaming.

I sit up, my heart racing. It's darker in our room than the inside of a tunnel. Where's the night-light? I can't see a thing.

Who is that screaming?

It's Jen.

"What happened? Are you hurt?" I shout and I remember the crash. Has the roof caved in? All that heavy snow. Oh no! Did it fall on Jen? Is she hurt?

She's not screaming anymore but she's whimpering, and that's almost worse.

I try to get out of my sleeping bag, but I can't see and I'm all tangled up.

"Mr. Webster," I scream, clawing out of the bag. "Somebody, help!" I'm stumbling across the floor, feeling in the dark for Jen's bed.

I didn't need to scream, because her parents are already coming. They're calling, "It's all right, sweetheart. It's all right."

Our door is partway open, and there's a bright, moving beam of light in the hallway outside. Now I can see. Jen's sitting up. I can tell she's terrified, and she's still making those little mewling sounds. Nothing has fallen on her. The roof's still there, safe and solid over her head.

I stand back, because Mr. and Mrs. Webster are holding her, kneeling next to the bed. Jen's got the big flashlight, its beam shaking and weaving against the wooden walls.

I'm really mystified. "What happened?" I whisper to Mr. Webster.

"The storm toppled a tree. It knocked out the electricity. But it's all right. We have an emergency lantern in the car. I'll go get it, Jen. You keep the flashlight."

"I couldn't find mine," she wails. "It was under my pillow."

I see it on the floor and give it to her. She switches it on so she has two, one in each hand, and all the time her mom is murmuring to her, stroking her hair.

I can't understand what's going on. "The tree didn't fall on the cabin, did it?" I whisper.

"No. Nothing like that."

I don't think I should ask anything else. Maybe Jen just had a bad dream after those spooky stories we told.

Mr. Webster has come back with the lantern. It's the kind that has a big, square battery on the bottom and looks like it could last forever. He sets it on the stool, next to the key ring and the postcard Jen had written for Izzy. It lights up the room, white and shadowless.

Jen slumps down in her sleeping bag and gives me a wavery smile.

"We'll leave the light," her dad tells her. "Unless you girls want to bring your stuff and come sleep on the floor of our room."

"No, it's O.K." Jen reaches out for my hand. "I have the light. And Callie's here."

"Callie? Will you be able to sleep? It's so bright in here," Mrs. Webster asks.

"I'll be fine," I say.

They stay for a while.

Mrs. Webster brings me another glass of water. That's the third tonight. "How are you, Honey?" she asks. "Feeling better?"

I nod. "Yes, thanks."

After they've gone, we stay quiet for a few minutes. Then Jen says in the smallest voice, "I'm such a baby, Callie. I'm so scared of the dark. I hate to tell anybody. I mean, I know the dark is just like the light . . ."

"Except that it's dark," I add, and Jen gives a little gulpy giggle.

"Exactly. There's a friend of my mom's. She's a kind of doctor and she's helping me. She says I'll get over this. But I'm not there yet."

I nod. I have to say it now. I have to. I take a deep breath. "I'm scared to death of heights," I say in my own small voice. I wait for some kind of lightning to strike as the words fill the little room. I've

said it out loud. But there's nothing except the roar of the wind outside.

"Was that what made you sick today?" Jen asks.

"That and the altitude. I'm not sure about the altitude part, though," I add. "But I hate it that I spoiled everything for you."

"You didn't. I'm just glad you came. You were brave to try, Callie."

"I was resolved," I tell her.

We're quiet again. I don't know if Jen's asleep or not.

"You know what?" I say. "I bet everybody's afraid of something. Even Izzy."

"Well, she's definitely afraid about her parents breaking up," Jen says. "But that's not exactly the same thing." We lie, pondering.

"But she could have a secret fear," I suggest.

"Like us," Jen says.

"Yep. You know my brother, Tom? He's scared of clowns. But you can't tell anyone. I don't think he'd mind me telling you, since this is a kind of emergency. He says if he saw a clown he'd run and hide behind a stack of baked beans."

"Baked beans?" Jen laughs out loud, and her laugh sounds so good.

"Honest. That's what he told me."

We don't talk anymore. The wind isn't so fierce now, and there's a kind of everywhere hush.

I'm thinking about Monster Mountain. Snow could be falling on it right now, soft and silky. Will I ever be able to even look at it and not be afraid? Will I ever be able to snowboard down it? Will Jen ever ask me to come up here with her again? So many questions, and I don't know any of the answers. If Jen doesn't ask me, will she ask Izzy? How will that make me feel? I don't know the answer to that, either. I do know that tonight has made Jen and me even closer friends than we were before. We're tighter. It's like nothing could change that.

I reach out for the key ring and hold it tight. When I get home, I'm going to tell Izzy that Jen and I have decided we're going to read *A Wrinkle in Time* next. She should get it so the three of us can read it at the same time. I think that will be a good start.